P9-CCZ-072

*I was born in a* shtetl, *a little Jewish town in Russia, many years ago. Times were hard for the Jews there, and when I was six months old my father left for America to make a better life for our family. It took him almost seven years of hard work to save enough money to bring my mother and me to America to join him. So I spent the first seven years of my life with my mother in our little town of Wysokie, without my father. Sometimes I would cry because my father was so far away, but he sent us letters and money and pictures of himself and that made me feel better. This story is about my memories of those years, and of my last days before leaving for America.*

אין אָנדענק פון מיין יידיש שטעטעלע וויסאָקע ליטעווסק,
וואָס איז מער נישטאָ, און געהייליקט מיין משפחה וואָס איז
דאָרטן אומגעקומען צוזאַמען מיט אַלע יידן.

Dedication:

To the memory of all the people of Wysokie-Litewskie who are no more
and most of all to my beloved family who perished with them.

*I would like to thank my husband George Perry for his constant
help and encouragement.*

*Roslyn Bresnick-Perry*

In loving memory of my parents who gave me the gift of life and the love of
learning and for Dorothy who taught me the magic of silent reading.

*I would like to thank Rayna Zussman and family, Alana Traynor and family, Melissa Levin,
Glenn Hirsh, Heidi Denton, Joyce Harada, Cheryl Dugan, Loralie Mansur, Susan Kirschenbaum and
Jack Ostrofsky, Armagh Cassil, Elly Simmons and John Cook, Victoria Kauffman for photo on page 32,
Nina Raff, Michael Shapiro, Dottie Myers and Dorothy Coakley of the Bernal Heights Library,
Roland and Carla and the staff at Orr Hot Springs, Collette Gelade, Norma and Bernard Schecter,
Harriet Rohmer and David Schecter and the Judah Magnes Museum.*

*Mira Reisberg*



The Yiddish words in this book are transliterated according to the
standard scheme of the YIVO Institute for Jewish Research.

 Editors: Harriet Rohmer and David Schecter Design: Mira Reisberg Production: Tony Yuen Photography: Lee Fatherree
Children's Book Press is a nonprofit community publisher. Printed in Hong Kong through Interprint.

Library of Congress Cataloging-in-Publication Data
Bresnick-Perry, Roslyn. Leaving for America / Story by Roslyn Bresnick-Perry : pictures by Mira Reisberg. p. cm.
Summary: The author recalls her early years in a small Jewish town in western Russia and the last days there as she and her mother prepare to join her father in the United States.
1. Bresnick-Perry, Roslyn—Juvenile literature. 2. Jews-Belarus-Wysokie—Biography—Juvenile literature. 3. Wysokie (Belarus)—Biography—Juvenile literature. 4. Soviet Union—Emigration and immigration—Biography—Juvenile literature. [1. Bresnick-Perry, Roslyn. 2. Jews—Soviet Union. 3. Soviet Union—Emigration and immigration. 4. United States—Emigration and immigration.]
I. Reisberg, Mira, ill. II. Title. DS135.R95B6954 1992 947'.652—dc20 [B] 92-8450 CIP AC

**Children's Book Press San Francisco & Emeryville, California**

# LEAVING FOR AMERICA

Story by Roslyn Bresnick-Perry
Pictures by Mira Reisberg

We were leaving for America. My mother and I were leaving our *shtetl*, our little town of Wysokie, to join my father. Everyone had been talking about our going for so long that I thought the time would never come, but here it was, the very day.

We had said goodbye to friends, relatives and neighbors two or three times each because we kept meeting them on the street or in the marketplace or at the synagogue. We had said goodbye so often that my mother finally stopped crying at each farewell.

I was sad to be leaving everyone, but something inside of me kept bubbling up with excitement and I couldn't keep myself from smiling even though everyone else seemed so heavy-hearted.

Everyone made such a fuss over us. They invited us to have tea and cookies. They gave us advice and told my mother what to do and what not to do, who to get in touch with and who to be careful of.

"There are so many thieves in America," they said. They knew because their uncle or cousin or brother or sister who was there wrote to them about it. Everyone taught us the few words of English they knew. "You say 'yes' for *yo*, 'no' for *neyn* and 'okay' for everything else."

Chocolate Matzos
GROCERIES
KOSHER
Pepsi-Cola is sanctioned for Passover Use by the Union of Orthodox Jewish Congregations of America.
Pepsi-Cola
Kosher for Passover
כשר לפסח
5¢
HOKAY
STRICTLY KOSHER
SAMSTEIN'S
כשר כשר
MEAT & POULTRY MARKET

I said goodbye to my cousin Zisl when we left our house and went to stay with my grandmother and grandfather for the final few days before we were due to leave for America. My mother wanted to be with them until the very last moment because she had a terrible feeling we would never see them again.

I knew I would really miss Zisl. She was my best and worst friend. Sometimes we would love each other and sometimes we would fight. She used to get me into all kinds of trouble because she had so many ideas.

One time Zisl found a can of dark green paint and she wanted me to help her paint our old outhouse. I was wearing the new dress my father had sent me from America. "Oh, I can't!" I cried. "My dress will get dirty and my mother will kill me!"

But Zisl had an answer right on the spot. "You can take off your dress and paint in your underwear."

"But everyone will see me in my underwear," I said, "and that's not nice."

"No, they won't either," said Zisl. "I'll watch out for you. Come on, stop being a cry baby. Let's go."

I got a good spanking for that adventure.

Zisl's family lived right next door to us. We used to tell each other all our secrets. I told her how I saw my Aunt Feygl kissing her boyfriend Srolke when she was supposed to be taking care of me. Everybody knew this was not allowed when you weren't married.

Right away Zisl got a gleam in her eye and said, "Let's tell Srolke that we're going to let the whole family know what they were doing unless he gives us a ride in his horse-drawn sleigh."

But Aunt Feygl and Srolke were getting married right after that so they didn't care if everyone knew they were kissing. Srolke promised he would take us for a ride some day, but Zisl and I both knew he was always too busy to bother with us.

We never got our ride, but we had fun anyway by telling each other our dreams about flying to the moon in Srolke's sleigh. Zisl's dream was better than mine and I didn't like that at all. But afterwards I didn't care so much. I knew I would miss Zisl a lot.

HOMAGE A CHAGALL

On the day we were leaving for America, I woke up very early in the morning. A horse and wagon were already waiting for us at my grandparents' door. Grandfather and my uncle Avrom-Leyb, my mother's youngest brother, were carrying a large steamer trunk out of the house. Inside the trunk was everything that we were taking to America.

My mother had a hard time deciding what to take. She finally came to the conclusion that in America it would be impossible to get a feather bed like hers or the kind of linens she liked or such lovely embroidered underwear she was used to wearing, so she took all she had. She also took her copper pots and pans and her two silver candlesticks. Then when everything was packed, she put in her two wooden rolling pins, one on each side of the trunk.

קינדער
בוך

Those rolling pins later created a sensation by falling out of the trunk during the many immigration inspections we had to undergo upon arriving in America. The inspectors asked my mother if she had brought them along to use on her husband. Then they laughed and laughed at their own joke. We just stood there not knowing why they were laughing. When the joke was finally explained to my mother she looked even more puzzled than before.

"Do women really hit their husbands with rolling pins in America?" she asked. "What a crazy land, America!"

Ha ha ha
ha ha
ha h
UNITED STATES IMMIGRATION
Ha Ha Ha
haha
????
ha
US
HA ha
ha ha ha
Ha Ha
Ha ha ha

On the morning we left for America, however, everything rested quietly in the trunk which Grandfather and Avrom-Leyb had loaded onto the wagon. I ran outside to watch every detail of what was going on. Everyone was crying. My mother, my Aunt Shuske and my grandmother were standing by the wagon with their arms around each other, weeping without restraint. My Aunt Libe was in the house crying her eyes out. Aunt Feygl and Srolke cried silently, wiping their eyes and nose every few minutes. My grandfather comforted me, but he too was crying, his tears rolling out without a sound into his curly, honey-colored beard.

Seeing all the people of my world crying propelled me into hysterical sobbing. I cried the loudest although only a few minutes before I had been filled with laughter and excitement. My grandmother, hearing my cries, tore herself out of my mother's arms, ran into the house and was back in what seemed like a minute carrying a large slice of rye bread heaped high with chopped liver.

"*Na Mamele, es epis,*" she said. "Now darling, eat a little something so you'll feel better."

I ate my chopped liver crying with much less emotion. After all, how emotional can you be while eating chopped liver?

Everything was now ready for our departure. My mother had finally freed herself from all those loving arms and was sitting on the passenger seat of the wagon waiting for me. It was time to say goodbye to my grandfather.

I loved my grandfather. He was a tall, handsome, gentle man who always had a twinkle in his eyes and a smile on his lips whenever he saw me. Grandfather helped me learn my *Alef Beys*, my ABCs. He said that I must learn my letters so that I could read the Holy Books and the history of our people, and grow up knowing what is right and who I am.

Now it was time for us to leave. My grandfather reached over and started to lift me up to my mother in the wagon. But when I was in mid-air he stopped and looked at me with great love and sadness.

"*Un du, mayn eynikl, du vest blaybn an emese yidishe tokhter?*" he whispered. "And you, my grandchild, will you remain a true Jewish daughter of your people?"

What a strange question, I thought, but I answered him cheerily. "*Avade, Zeyde*." "Of course, Grandfather."

חי
שלום

It has now been many years since the joyous day when my mother and I were reunited with my father in America. I am now a grandmother myself. But I have never forgotten my old home and all the wonderful people of my childhood. And I have never forgotten my grandfather's question.

## About **Leaving For America**

*I am a storyteller. I tell stories to preserve the memory of my family and the little Jewish town in Russia where I grew up. I tell stories of warm family relations, celebrations, mishaps, coincidences and intrigues. But mostly I tell of the comical adventures of two little girls, my cousin Zisl and myself, who grew up in another time, another world. When people ask me if I still see Zisl, I sadly must tell them that Zisl died in the Holocaust, when six million Jews were murdered in World War II. Then, all of a sudden, my audience becomes very quiet, because this thing that happened is not just "six million Jews," it's Zisl.*

*Stories are magical. They cross generations, they dissolve time and space, they overcome differences and barriers. You feel a connection, an empathy, a reaching out, when you hear someone's story. That's why we must share our stories with one another. And that is why I share mine with you.*

*Roslyn Bresnick-Perry*

Author Roslyn Bresnick-Perry was born in the little Russian Jewish town of Wysokie-Litewskie in 1922, and came to America with her mother in 1929. Her extended family perished in the Holocaust in World War II. She grew up in New York City and struggled to overcome her family tragedy, culture shock, a language barrier, and dyslexia. After 33 years working in the garment industry as a fashion designer, she graduated from college, completed an M.A. degree in Cultural History, and ultimately found her niche as a professional storyteller. Her audio tape, *Holiday Memories of a Shtetl Childhood*, has been honored by the American Library Association as a Notable Recording for Children. This is her first children's book.

Artist Mira Reisberg was born in Melbourne, Australia in 1955. When her mother gave Mira her first art supplies, she said, "I can't give you a beautiful world but you can make one for yourself." As the daughter of Holocaust survivors, Mira felt a close connection with Roslyn's story. The family pictures in the book include Mira's family as well as Roslyn's. Mira used mixed media to illustrate *Leaving For America*, keeping the feel of the time but adding her own more contemporary colors. This is Mira's fourth book with Children's Book Press. Her previous books include *Uncle Nacho's Hat* (a UNICEF award winner and Reading Rainbow Selection), *Baby Rattlesnake* (A Sesame Street Read Along), and *Elinda Who Danced in the Sky*.